# YOU CAN

Playing Subbuteo on a Friday night with his elder brother Mick is the highlight of David's week. It doesn't even really matter that on this particular Friday, Mick gets home first and so has the choice of being Spurs. But, little does either boy realize that this Friday is to be the last of these happy games. For soon everything is to change – Mum and Dad split up and Mick, now at a new school and with new friends, has no time for his younger brother. So, when David gets his chance in the school soccer team, he wonders whether there will be anyone to share his big day.

Chris Ashley, like his author-father Bernard, is a keen football supporter. He teaches at a junior school in Bury, Lancashire, where he lives with his wife and two young sons. *You Can Be Spurs* was his first published book.

Also by Chris Ashley

*Songs on the South Bank*
(Published by Julia MacRae Books)

# You can be Spurs

## Chris Ashley

*Illustrated by*
John Dillow

WALKER BOOKS
LONDON

First published 1989 by Julia MacRae Books
This edition published 1990 by
Walker Books Ltd, 87 Vauxhall Walk
London SE11 5HJ

Typeset in Hong Kong by Graphicraft Typesetters Ltd
Printed in Great Britain by
Richard Clay Ltd, Bungay, Suffolk

British Library Cataloguing in Publication Data
Ashley, Chris
You can be spurs.
I. Title   II. Dillow, John
823'.914 [J]
ISBN 0-7445-1748-6

# Contents

*For Marlene*

# *1* Who will be spurs?

Friday afternoon three-thirty, and David Taylor sat up iron-straight, arms folded, eyes popping and every muscle strained in an effort to show how ready to go home he was.

Mrs Graham wasn't looking. Time to re-arrange his pencil case on top of his reading book and cast a critical eye over the other members of the group. He might have known. "Shut-up Ackland," he hissed.

A purple Ryan Ackland was in exactly the same vessel-bursting position, but being Ryan Ackland he had also decided not to breathe and was making 'Look at me' noises so that Mrs Graham would see how he deserved to be first.

"Umm, this is a second year class not a zoo, Green group, and I'm looking for the quietest children."

Mrs Graham hadn't even looked to see who the animal imitator was. Getting the message and unable to survive any longer, the shuddering Ryan Ackland emptied his lungs and gulped in fresh oxygen in an explosion of sound.

The whole of class 2G turned to look and Mrs Graham raised a warning eyebrow. That had really blown it. Friday night was *Subbuteo* night and this

was a bad start. David Taylor had to get home before his brother so that he could decide which team to be.

It was no good explaining that to Ackland. He wouldn't understand. Anyway there was no chance now.

And just to confirm his worst fears, a gaggle of sound filled the corridors of Moss Lane Junior and rushing shapes darkened the frosted glass which was separating David from freedom and his race for home.

As he looked, a face pressed against the glass and took on the form of a grinning Michael Taylor, David's brother from the fourth year. The shape's hand came up beside his face and started performing a strange movement.

At first David couldn't see what it was he was doing. Then he realised and he had to laugh. Just like Mick he was rubbing it in, flicking an imaginary *Subbuteo* man to show that he would get to the box of players first. He would be Spurs.

David smiled to himself as the figure at the window faded away. Oh well, at least it was Friday. He'd beat Mick anyway.

Finally free, David crashed through the school doors and sprinted the two streets to home.

Not bothering with the front door, he rushed round the back and through the kitchen. Kicking two pairs of football boots away from the mat and flinging his bag into a corner, he was banging up the stairs before a tired and cross-looking Mrs Taylor emerged from the front room where, still wearing her Tesco's overall, she had been dozing in front of an Australian soap opera.

"I work my fingers to the bone for two sons and not one of them can be bothered to even say 'hello' to me. Where are you going in such a hurry?"

"Hello Mum, playing *sub*."

David didn't wait for a reply, he launched himself at Mick's bedroom door. Perhaps the elder boy would have made a mistake and could be in the toilet or getting his football kit out of the airing cupboard ready for the school match tomorrow; the rules were clear. Whoever was there first chose the teams.

No chance!

Mick was sitting, cross-legged, pulling a funny face in an exact take-off of David and Ryan Ackland's 'ready to go home position'. In front of him, instead of a desk and a reading book was a bright green carpet with eleven tiny, plastic men in position for the kick-off of a football match. Every miniature player was skilfully painted in white shirts, blue shorts and white socks.

"Please Miss," said Michael in a little child's voice, "can I go home?"

David went hot with the embarrassment at having been seen as a goody-goody in class. "You rotten..."

He didn't get the chance to finish the sentence, because Michael had gone into the next stage of his act and was now making 'Mmm...mmm... mmm' Ryan Ackland 'Look at me' noises.

David rose to the bait just as Michael knew he would and, tongue between teeth, dived at the bigger boy, arms flailing and legs kicking. But Michael was much stronger and waiting for the attack. With one movement he pushed his growling brother off and crashed him to the floor, knocking the wind out of him and making the floor shudder.

He was on David's chest and in the act of stuffing a dirty sock into his mouth, when the door burst open and there was Mum, scarlet with anger, her throat too tight for words to come.

"You kids ..!" It was all she could manage, and the boys knew this was serious. Michael immediately rolled off David and pulled him into a sitting position.

"Sorry Mum, we were only playing."

"As if I haven't got enough problems. Neither of you bothered to say hello, I haven't seen your dad for two days and I'm expected to keep this house going."

"Sorry, Mum."

"Yeah, sorry Mum," joined David, "but he was . . ."

"I'm not interested. That game causes more arguments than anything in this house. One of these days I'm going to throw the whole box into the dustbin."

She ran out of breath and her mind seemed to go somewhere else. The boys glanced at each other. She was calming down now.

After an age, she sighed. "Anyway, what do you want for tea?"

"Anything thanks, Mum," said Michael, relieved that he seemed to be off the hook.

David wasn't so easily pleased.

"It's Friday, Mum. Dad'll bring home fish and chips."

For some reason this seemed to cause another flair up.

"You have what you're given, my boy. I haven't seen your father in two days." She was on her way out of the room now and back on the stairs.

The boys smirked at each other again and gave a thumbs up sign. They'd got away with it.

"He's not going to swan in here with his fish and chips and expect everything to be all right," came a distant voice from below. "If he brings fish and chips in here, I'll throw them straight into the dustbin."

"If there's room next to the *Subbuteo* men," whispered David and both boys collapsed laughing on the floor until the kitchen door slammed shut and the game could finally start.

# 2 Changes

*Subbuteo.*

*Table Top Soccer*, the makers called it, even though David and Michael played it on the carpet.

'Stupid Kids' game' was Mum's name for it, especially when she'd just trodden barefoot on a player left on the floor. But then she was always moaning these days.

In the hands of experts, though, the game became the real thing – better even, sometimes.

The matches always took place up in Mick's room and for hour after knee-breaking hour the boys would lean over the green cloth pitch as the tiny figures being flicked at a small ball became the world's great players and the bedroom became a crowded stadium staging the most important matches in soccer history.

Tonight was no different. Mick was Spurs, but because David couldn't bear to be anyone else he had chosen some yellow players and called his team Old Spurs and named his men after some players his dad had told him about, like Jimmy Greaves and Pat Jennings.

Soon, all arguments forgotten, both boys were completely absorbed in the matches, only stopping to stretch their aching backs or to search for the ball when it had been whacked under the bed.

Each match lasted for six minutes, the three minutes of each half measured with the heart-stopping sands of an egg-timer. Arguments flared and died down, especially as panic set in when the sand ran out at the end of each game. It was worse in one game when, with only seconds to go, Mick, a goal up, 'accidentally on purpose' caused one of his men to kick the ball right under the wardrobe and Mum called them down to tea before a frantic David could fish the ball out and get it back into play.

He didn't mind too much though, Mick was a good brother and he was much fairer to him than the brothers some of the other kids had got. Nicky Park's brother never played with him and everybody was scared of Ryan Ackland's elder brother; no wonder Ryan acted like a twit in school. It was the only way to get anybody to notice him.

At the table the brothers started talking excitedly about their tournament, which was reaching a climax, but Mum just sat there hardly touching the food she had made. She had been crying and the

more sensitive Mick nudged David and signalled him to be quiet.

"What's up, Mum?" he asked, going to her and putting an arm around her shoulders. She held his hand there but said nothing.

"Where's Dad?" piped up David, but Mick silenced him with a look and David went back to his fish fingers.

They were washing up when a rap at the window told them that Mr Taylor was home.

"How's my lads?" he asked. "Got a game tomorrow, son?"

Mick nodded and a proud Dad ruffled his hair.

"You going to come and watch too, Davy boy? We'll practise your heading again behind the goal."

Things were back to normal; the large, cheerful frame of John Taylor had changed the mood in the kitchen just as David had seen him do at family parties or when he was standing with his team-mates at the club bar after his Sunday side had lost.

David looked round to draw his mum in with the happier mood. But she had gone.

John Taylor was looking in the same direction and for a split second his wide smile and sparkling eyes had died. But only for a second.

"I bet I know what you boys are up to. Come on, finish washing up and I'll take you both on. I'll show you what Spurs were like when they had a real team."

The rest of the evening had been great. Dad had played with them and David and Michael joined together to oppose him.

Dad wasn't as practised as the boys, but he was good at commentating and he gave the matches a fantastic atmosphere. In the end, Dad's team of old stars had lost by about twelve to sixteen but the score didn't really matter, the boys had enjoyed showing off their skills.

When it got late the three went laughing downstairs and enjoyed crisps and peanuts in front of the television.

David was too tired to notice that Mum and Dad didn't exchange a single word and though later, when he was in bed, he heard the banging and shouts from downstairs, he was still too tired to wonder what they were or to let them disturb him.

That Friday was the end of something. Saturday had started normally enough; David got up and put on his football kit and tracksuit and went with Mick and Dad up to the school playing fields.

He had watched with his normal envy as Mick and the rest of the team put on their red and blue tops and then he had rushed on to the pitch with Dad to listen to the bit of last minute advice that the expert Mr Taylor always gave his son.

It was usually something like, "Get that first tackle in hard, son... Let them know you're there." Or, "Look for your men, play the simple ball."

David knew that Mick was secretly proud of their dad coming on and often the other lads would listen and then echo his advice amongst themselves. "Play the simple ball – play the simple ball."

Today, though, Dad did something completely different. Instead of talking he crouched down and suddenly put his arms around both boys and fiercely pulled them towards him. It was a shock. David never forgot how tight Dad held them, how his stubble rubbed their faces and actually hurt, or how Dad's breath smelt of drink as he whispered. He didn't understand what Dad meant at the time. But he soon would.

"Whatever happens, you two, stick together. Look after each other – look after Mum... Now go on Micky, win your match."

Then Dad kissed them, put his hands in the pockets of his leather bomber jacket and trotted to the side-line.

A scarlet Mick had avoided the shocked looks from his team-mates and, hands on hips, got into position for the kick-off.

David had just stood there, looking at Dad and it took a shout from Mr Harris, the football teacher, to get him off the pitch and out of the way.

The game kicked off and as always the two Moss Lane forwards side-footed the ball to each other and then passed it back to Mick who, with his usual skill, pumped the ball high into the other team's half. A perfect start.

David cheered and Mr Taylor nodded. He put his arm round David and squeezed his shoulder. David cheered again and ran up the touch-line to see if Moss Lane could turn the opening attack into

a goal, and they almost did, only a save from the goalkeeper preventing a fierce shot from going in.

A corner anyway. David looked back to see what advice Dad was giving. But Dad wasn't there. Shoulders hunched, hands still in pockets, he was walking through the gates and out of sight.

Dad had gone!

And in the next six months the boys saw him just once, an awkward day out with few real words spoken, and someone Dad called Auntie Carol trying to be funny by wearing a silly hat they'd been given in the hamburger bar.

David knew he'd lost Dad after the day out and he cried real tears in bed that night. Mum came and sat with him, but Mick didn't. It was the first sign he could remember that told David he'd lost someone else, too.

# *3* In the team

"And now I think you've got something exciting to show us, haven't you Mr Harris?"

David stopped picking at the rubber bottom of his training shoe and, like everybody else in the hall, twisted his neck to get a better view of the large bearded man lumbering to his feet. In his hands were two mysterious white boxes. Eyes shone. The two hundred and fifty children of Moss Lane Junior school were willing him to finish their Friday afternoon assembly with something really good.

It had been a happy occasion already: Miss Disney had been in one of her jokey moods, and now they were ready to pay her back by being excited with what Mr Harris had to show. There might even be the chance for a loud cheer, and a few secret nods between older children said they were ready to risk starting one as soon as the boxes revealed their secret.

Not so long ago David would have been one of them. But now he ignored the nudging of Nicky Parks next to him and turned his attention back to

the growing pile of rubber by his crossed legs. He thought back to Friday afternoons last year. He used to love Fridays: beefburgers for school dinner; afternoon assembly with some work to show, and then running home for the big game with Mick.

Over the last six months David had played *Subbuteo* with other boys, with friends from school and cubs. But other kids didn't commentate as if it was real, and they had different rules. No, it was never the same as the Taylors' Friday game: Mick describing the action for the T.V. cameras and him providing the gasps and cheers of a massive crowd. It was great! And even though the evening often ended with one of them storming out of the room after losing a big cup tie, they'd soon make up and get down to picking what teams they wanted for the next competition.

David heaved a silent sigh and collected all of his bits of rubber with the edge of his hand. If only it could be the same now, he thought, he would even let Mick choose the white shirts. "Go on," he'd say generously, "you can be Spurs." Mr Harris had started talking now but David wasn't listening. His mind was still on the old *Subbuteo* days. So what had changed? Well, Dad had gone, but why wasn't there anything to look forward to any more .. ?

The answer to that was easy. David blasted his pile of rubber in disgust. Mick had changed. A few months after leaving Moss Lane to go to the Senior School and the kind big brother now seemed a sneering bully. The brother who'd been such a close friend before their dad left had found different friends: hard-faced boys who David remembered causing trouble at the swimming baths

last summer. Both brothers had stayed well away then, but now Mick had got in with them and all he wanted to do was try and look tough like they did. Mick's room, once the scene of so much fun, was a no-go area now and going in meant a hard kick, the real kind.

A cheer from the school hall and another nudge from Nicky snapped David back to what Mr Harris was saying. "They've done very well and tomorrow morning we'll be on the field bright and early to see if we can beat Hale Manor and win a trophy for our school."

Of course, the football. The fourth year team had won all their matches and had got a place in the Borough Cup Final. Everyone was going to watch and the mayor was going to give the cup away. David perked up and began to pay attention. He was only a third year, but it could be him in it next year; he'd definitely be good enough to play for the school then. Already some people said he was the best third year they had.

"Stand up those boys who are playing," said Mr Harris. "Let's wish them good luck for tomorrow, shall we?"

Twelve fourth year boys pulled themselves lazily
to their feet and tried not to smile as a great cheer
rang round the old hall. Miss Disney finally
stopped it by putting a finger to her lips. "Don't
keep us in suspense any longer, Mr Harris. What's
in those lovely boxes?"

Mr Harris pulled a special face and, like a
magician on the television, he angled the boxes
towards the hushed hall: then with a great wizard's
sweep of his arm, he took the lid off the top one.
Slowly, with a rustle of tissue paper, he brought
out a blue and red striped football shirt: short

sleeves, v-neck collar, with something special in the material that made it shine. There were some in the hall who looked at each other in disappointment: the surprise didn't concern them. But the twelve standing up stared open-mouthed at the boxes,

their reward for getting through to the final: and on the floor, David felt his heart miss a beat as he went through a great pang of jealousy. What wouldn't he give to wear a shirt like that? Red and blue in the school colours, but more than a school kit. This was a Barcelona strip! The exact style! David's stomach turned as he imagined what it would be like to wear one of those shirts: and then hugging his knees, he had to settle for hoping that the fourth years wouldn't spoil them before it was his turn to wear one next year.

David was doing battle at the classroom door, trying to get out for home, when he heard the shouts coming from the corridor. An extra push and he was soon in the crowd around Steven Tuckey, white-faced and shaking and hating the attention that had come from being violently sick. He was a terrific footballer, one of the twelve, and West Ham were supposed to be interested in him. Without his goals, Moss Lane would never have got through to tomorrow's final.

"Move away you lot!" Mr Harris broke through the crowd and stepped over the mess to get to the miserable boy, who was suddenly ill again. "Let's

get you home," he said, putting a hand gingerly on the boy's shoulder.

"Tuckey won't be able to play tomorrow, will he, sir?" came a helpful voice from the crowd.

"What? We'll see." But the look on Mr Harris's face said it all. David had never seen him look so choked.

"We haven't got a chance, have we, sir? Tuckey gets all our goals."

Mr Harris ignored the voice of doom and marched off towards a telephone with Steven Tuckey following a few steps behind, while David carefully picked his own way down the corridor to begin his Friday night. Already he was planning how not to get home until Mick had gone out with his mates – when Mr Harris suddenly turned.

"It's David, isn't it?"

"Yes, Mr Harris."

"Listen, son, are you doing anything tomorrow morning? I've seen you at Football Club. You're a natural attacker." He dropped his voice. "Steven's not going to be fit and Ian, our sub, is a bit slow to put up front. Could you play for us in the final?"

David shot a look at Tuckey, who really was too

ill to care. "Yeah! – I mean yes, Mr Harris."

"Right. Nine-thirty outside the gates. Don't be late."

"No, sir!"

David forgot all about delaying going home. He ran the three streets, jumping and heading imaginary goals all the way. This was it! His luck had changed! Stragglers had heard Mr Harris ask him to play, and already he felt like a star. Ryan

Ackland's gang had said, "Well done, Dave," and even Linda Jones had given him a smile and winked, "Do your best." She'd hardly even spoken to him before and she definitely wasn't interested in football. This Cup Final had to be an even bigger thing than he'd thought. And he didn't need to think about what to do on his Friday night now. It would take him all evening to get his kit ready. He and Mick could clean their boots together. Mick always scrubbed his rugby boots on a Friday before playing for the seniors on a Saturday morning.

David's mind raced. In fact, Mick and his mates always cut back across the Moss Lane field after their matches. Last time the Moss Lane football team had played on a Saturday, the seniors had put their bags down and stood behind one of the goals singing songs like a real football crowd. Now David could picture it. Mick leading a gang behind the posts and watching his younger brother score the winning goal, volleyed in from a low cross.

"That's my brother. I taught him that," Mick would say – and then start the singing: "There's only one David Taylor, there's only one David Taylor!" And even if David didn't score, Mick would have to be secretly proud of him getting a medal from the mayor.

But all that would have to wait until tomorrow. Mick was already in when David got home and David's cheerful shout of "Mickey, clean your boots for you? I'm playing for the school tomorrow," was answered with, "Shut up!" and "What do they want *you* for? That school's really gone downhill since I played for them. You've only got one decent player. That Tuckey kid."

David swallowed his disappointment and went to

the cupboard under the stairs to find his own kit. Red shorts and boots; and he would borrow Mick's red socks. He cheered up and thought he'd try again, because the old Mick would have been really pleased for him. "Can I borrow your red socks,

Mick? You should see the kit old Harris has bought us. Barcelona, red and blue stripes."

But instead of a reply two heavy objects hit him in the small of the back and really hurt – David doubled up on the floor as the scowling boy came banging down the stairs.

"Yes and no... Yes, you can clean my boots. No, you can't borrow my socks. What's the point of old Harris buying a new kit when he's only got rubbish like you to wear it?" Mick reached the bottom step and picked up his bomber jacket from the bannister. "Get up! That didn't hurt. You can't play for the school if you can't take a bit of pain!"

The front door slammed and David was left holding his back, not knowing whether to cry or not. He went to the kitchen and found the boot polish and allowed himself to think back to when Mick had played for Moss Lane Juniors.

Dad had been there then; David remembered him polishing Mick's boots and saying, "Don't forget boys. Look after your boots and they'll look after you." That was a footballer talking. What would he have said about his third year son playing for the school?

He'd have been there tomorrow, shouting from the line: you couldn't have kept him away. But who was going to be there for him now?... Mick, probably, after his rugby match. Just there to make fun of him.

David's throat really hurt now. He heaved a

great sob and couldn't stop a tear splashing onto Mick's rugby boot. As it plopped onto the leather, an old piece of dried clod turned into brown mud which for a second smelt of a football pitch. The park, Anfield, Wembley: the feeling of excitement for the big match came back. *"There's only one David Taylor!"* Another tear fell but David quickly brushed it aside. He was in the mood again now. Wait until tomorrow. He'd show 'em.

# *4*  The Final

Saturday morning started cold but sunny and after splashing his face and running a comb through his hair, David set off, a piece of toast in his hand. He took the long way to school, putting on a footballer's limp as he walked importantly past the sleeping houses of Moss Lane, secretly hoping that an early riser would see him on his way to bring glory to their local school.

Much too early, he had a lot of hanging about to do. He'd gone to get a Mars bar from the corner shop which sold everything from toys to bin-liners, and then had a nasty few minutes hiding when Mick and his rugby mates climbed the school gates on their short cut across the field. He didn't want to get laughed at, or punched for wearing Mick's red socks. But at last Ben Weston turned up, the first of the fourth year team.

"What? Are you playing?"

"Yeah, Steven Tuckey's ill. Sir asked me."

"No! You any good then?"

"Not bad."

"Oh." Ben Weston didn't seem too sure. He walked to the corner to look out for other arrivals. Now cars started to come with boys yelping and

cheering, some already changed and some in tracksuits, all clustered in groups. David realised he didn't really know any of these boys and he felt a real idiot sitting on the wall. He ought to be with his team mates. So he edged down and stood on the fringe of Ben's group: but the excited crowd ran off to meet another car and David was alone again at the kerb. This wasn't how he'd pictured it! How could you feel so lonely with so many people around you?

At last, feeling a great wave of affection for Mr Harris's Ford Escort, he joined the rush to greet the teacher as he turned into the school road.

"Is it true we've got that Taylor kid instead of Steven Tuckey, sir? We haven't got a chance!"

David went a deep red, and his feeling of being an outsider made him long for his own home, Mick or no Mick.

"David Taylor's quite a good player," Mr Harris said, "for a third year. We'll have to make the best of it. Now then. Are we all here? Where's Ian? We've only got eleven; no sub."

"He said he's not turning up, sir, 'cos of Taylor playing instead of him."

Feeling worse than ever, David reached into his Sainsbury's bag and pulled out his boots. Secretly he spat on one and smelt the muddy leather to see if it gave him the same old feeling of excitement. It worked again. *I'll do my talking on the pitch*, he thought. *That's what Dad would have said.*

The gates finally opened and the excited crowd poured in, all Mr Harris's shouts of "Save your energy!" wasted on team members, who sprinted to the field and started kicking a ball almighty distances. Mr Harris caught up with them and brought the Moss Lane boys into a small circle for the team talk. Small puffs of steam came out of his mouth as he spoke into the cold air. A larger cloud followed as he breathed out heavily at the boys,

who were eyeing up the arrival of the Hale Manor team instead of listening. David had crouched down with the rest of the Moss Lane lads, and when they were told to warm up he saved himself the embarrassment of being left out of things again by kicking-in at the goalkeeper away from the rest.

Mr Harris finished shaking hands with a Hale Manor teacher, who looked every inch a football manager with his chewing gum and sheepskin coat, and called the boys back into a circle again.

Now he had the two white boxes with him. David could hardly believe he was actually going to wear one of those shirts. He put off the great moment of seeing the strip by looking at the scene around him: the touch-lines packed with chatting parents jumping and stamping to keep warm: a cluster of men putting a deck-chair down and then helping an elderly woman into it. He looked harder. She had a blanket round her knees, and a chain round her neck, and with a thrill of real excitement he knew that she must be the mayor. But there was more. A man in a tracksuit suddenly peeled it off to reveal a real black referee's outfit. There was a great wrenching in David's stomach.

For the first time he actually felt nervous about the
match. This was the business!

A huge cheer broke out from the lads, and David
allowed himself to look back again now and be
ready for his first glimpse of the blue and red
shirts.

But what he saw made his stomach drop like a boulder. The boxes still had their lids on, and nobody was looking at them at all. What they were looking at was a boy in a West Ham tracksuit – waving like mad as he jogged across the field towards them. A woman in a green coat was signalling to Mr Harris and in a daze, David saw Mr Harris's mouth moving, "Thanks Mrs Tuckey."

Another cheer broke out from the ring of boys, and David, who had been trying to focus on the white boxes in case this was all some trick of his

mind, had his dream broken by a sports bag being flung into the middle of the circle.

"All right, lads?"

Steven Tuckey was back, no trace of yesterday's illness, more at home in this circle on the grass than David had recently been in his own bedroom.

In a flash the boxes were open and the red and blue shirts were out. And David couldn't even swallow as he finally knew that he would not be getting one.

"I'll put you on at half-time, David," Mr Harris told him. "I've got to let Steven play. You understand, don't you?"

Yes, he understood. But David wondered if Mr Harris would have *had* to put Steven on if it had been his own dad on the line instead of the woman in the green coat. It wasn't fair!

David walked to the side and smiled bravely as tracksuit tops were thrown at him by boys looking like top professionals in their shiny stripes. Mr Harris went over and stood near the mayor and, without being told, David went with him. Well, he was still the substitute, wasn't he? He had to be near the teacher, ready to be sent on...

A loud whistle and the game began.

"Keep yourself warm, lad," Mr Harris said, but he soon forgot David as he got involved in shouting things to his players.

Hale Manor were a good side. They were big and confident, and their tackling left a few Moss Lane players wincing on the ground. But David wasn't bothered. As he saw the mud kicked up by the flying boots he longed to run on. He saw himself winning the ball and laying it off neatly to someone in blue and red. Even Steven Tuckey. Things were beginning to go badly for Moss Lane, and surely he could do better than they were at the moment, Hale Manor were all over them.

When Manor's first goal went in there were huge cheers from the other side of the pitch, and the shouting and advice from the grown-ups on the Moss Lane side became less friendly. But it didn't

do any good. The burly boys in their yellow shirts kept the ball in Moss Lane's half and by half-time they'd got another goal. Two-nil.

Mr Harris rushed on and David followed him to the half-way line, where the drooping shoulders underneath the new Moss Lane shirts told their own story. Was this it? He'd said half-time, hadn't he?

"I don't care how big they are! If you don't give them the ball they can't score can they? I haven't seen one of you get the ball to Steven Tuckey yet. You feed him and we'll score and then we're in with a chance. Now get out there and do it!" He marched back to the side-line, twenty metres from the mayor where he could shout as loud as he liked; and David ran at his heels.

"What about me, sir? Half-time, you said . . ."

"Yes, but I can't put you on yet. We'll see how it goes. We could still get back into this." He was talking to himself, not looking at David at all.

In the second half, Moss Lane did start getting to the ball first: and without the ball the big Hale Manor players looked less slick, and they soon began niggling at each other. Also, the odd ball

began getting through to Steven Tuckey. The crowd shouted when he got it. He was good. Even David forgot feeling sorry for himself and clapped him. Twice Steven had shots well saved by the goalkeeper, but on the third occasion a cross came to him on the edge of the penalty area, and he let the ball hit his thigh, then volleyed it towards the goal, just like the shot David had imagined scoring the night before. It was always going in – and parents rushed to Mr Harris's side and clapped him on the back. "We're back in it now all right!"

They stayed by the smiling teacher, as the unsmiling substitute found himself pushed away from the touch-line, looking at two grown-up backs. Now he couldn't see the pitch at all, and with a good chance of an equalizer coming, there was no chance he'd go on. David Taylor was out of it and he knew it.

For the third time since yesterday afternoon his throat hurt and his eyes prickled. He turned away from the pitch and through a mist of tears saw six big boys running towards him, flinging their sports bags into the air and singing, "Here we go, here we go, here we go."

One of them was Mick. "Oy! What are you doing in my socks? Come 'ere you!"

David had had enough. He turned away to face the grown-up backs and crouched down. He sensed somebody behind him and, sobbing, steeled himself to take what he had coming from his outraged brother.

What he got made the tears come even faster. A hand rested softly on his shoulder and an old familiar voice, a voice he hadn't heard in months asked him, "What's up, mate?"

David just went on sobbing. No words would come. Ages seemed to go by: then Mick pulled the smaller boy to him. Just like Dad had once done on the same field. "Hasn't he given you a game? He was always a so-and-so, old Harris."

A great cheer went up. Moss Lane had scored again. Two-all! An excited Mr Harris turned round and saw David. "Keep warm," he said, "I might bring you on in a minute."

Almost deafened by the noise, and not really able to see, the two brothers crouched on the line,

Mick's arm still around his younger brother. But ten minutes passed and Mr Harris didn't turn back. Time was running out now.

Finally another great bellow went around the school field. "Tuckey's done it again!" There were jumps and shouts everywhere, on the pitch and off. But Mick's hand stayed firm on David's shoulder.

"Moss Lane 3, Hale Manor 2. They've won it now!"

There was no time for more. Before the cheering had even died down, three blasts of the whistle shrilled that the game was over and an avalanche of people poured onto the pitch. Alone on the touch-line the Taylor boys stared at the excitement. Suddenly, Mick stiffened.

"Come on Dave, let's go," he said fiercely, and David felt himself being pushed through the shouting crowd by the shoulders, till he was away from the school and alone with his brother in the quiet outside the corner shop. The same shop he had visited a lifetime ago to buy a Mars.

"Wait here," Mick ordered as he went inside.

David looked back towards the school and heard the clapping echoing between the houses as the medals were given out.

"Close your eyes," a quiet voice ordered. It was Mick, and David did as he was told. Thrust into his hands was a rectangular box wrapped in paper. He opened his eyes.

"Cheers, Mick – chocolates?"

"You open it."

David took off the paper and for the hundredth time that day he felt his stomach roll. But this time it was with joy.

Looking up at him through the plastic window in

a green box were eleven tiny footballers, painted in blue and red stripes.

David stared at Mick and slowly broke into a wide grin. The elder boy looked at the ground and took a deep breath. "I'm sorry about...you know," Mick started.

David looked at him, and nodded. And suddenly he was running towards home, his Sainsbury's bag twirling around his head. "Come on," he shouted back, "you can be Spurs."

# MORE WALKER PAPERBACKS

## For You to Enjoy

| | | |
|---|---|---|
| ☐ 0-7445-1385-5 | *The Shape-Changer*<br>by Julian Atterton | £2.99 |
| ☐ 0-7445-1445-2 | *The Adventures of*<br>*Rama and Sita*<br>by Ruskin Bond | £2.99 |
| ☐ 0-7445-1749-4 | *Kick-Off*<br>by Hannah Cole | £2.99 |
| ☐ 0-7445-1419-3 | *Hetty's First Fling*<br>by Diana Hendry | £2.99 |
| ☐ 0-7445-1751-6 | *The Little Riders*<br>by Margaretha Shemin | £2.99 |
| ☐ 0-7445-1446-0 | *The Pepper Street*<br>*Papers*<br>by Joan Smith | £2.99 |
| ☐ 0-7445-1706-0 | *The Russian Doll*<br>by Joan Smith | £2.99 |
| ☐ 0-7445-1406-1 | *We Three Kings from*<br>*Pepper Street Prime*<br>by Joan Smith | £2.99 |